For Wiley, my friend and unconditional supporter

Reycraft Books
55 Fifth Avenue
New York, NY 10003
Reycraftbooks.com

Reycraft Books is a trade imprint and trademark of Newmark Learning, LLC.

Text and illustration copyright © 2019 by Wook Jin Jung

Library of Congress Cataloging-in-Publication Data is available.

ISBN: 978-1-4788-6816-3

Photo courtesy of Wook Jin Jung

Printed in Guangzhou, China
4401/0919/CA21901483
10 9 8 7 6 5 4 3 2 1
First Edition Hardcover published by Reycraft Books

BLACK CAT
YELLOW BUNNY

"Hello."

"Hi."

"Thank you."

Tuesday

"Good morning."

"Thank you."

"Thank you."

"Thank you."

"It's a very nice day."

"It sure is."

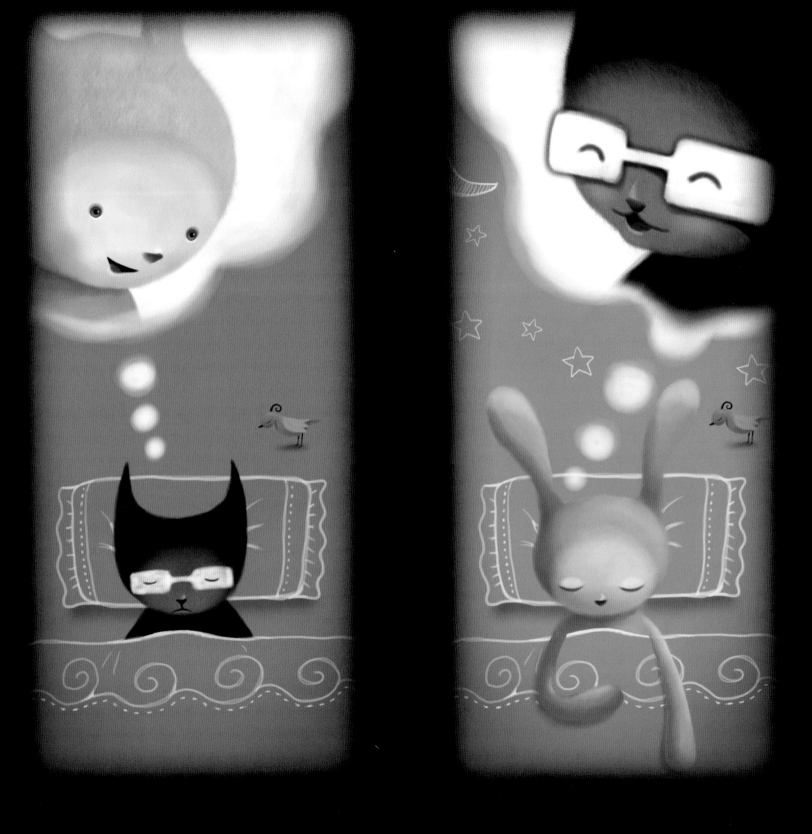

Saturday

"That's a pretty scarf."

"Thank you."

"Thank you!"